The 12 Days of Thanksgiving

by Jenna Lettice • illustrated by Colleen Madden

A Random House PICTUREBACK® Book

Random House 🏠 New York

Text copyright © 2018 by Jenna Lettice. Cover art and interior illustrations copyright © 2018 by Colleen Madden.
All rights reserved. Published in the United States by Random House Children's Books, a division of
Penguin Random House LLC, 1745 Broadway, New York, NY 10019. Pictureback, Random House,
and the Random House colophon are registered trademarks of Penguin Random House LLC.
rhcbooks.com
Library of Congress Control Number: 2017947926
ISBN 978-1-5247-6658-0 (trade) — ISBN 978-1-5247-6659-7 (ebook)
MANUFACTURED IN CHINA 10 9 8 7 6 5 4 3 2 1

On the **first** day
of Thanksgiving,
I was thankful for:

An evening at home
with family.

On the **second** day
of Thanksgiving,
I was thankful for:

Two sacks of apples
and an evening at home
with family.

On the **third** day
of Thanksgiving,
I was thankful for:

Three fall squash,
Two sacks of apples,
and an evening at home
with family.

On the **fourth** day
of Thanksgiving,
I was thankful for:

Four golden buckles,
Three fall squash,
Two sacks of apples,
and an evening at home
with family.

On the **fifth** day
of Thanksgiving,
I was thankful for:

Five piles of leaves!
Four golden buckles,
Three fall squash,
Two sacks of apples,
and an evening at home
with family.

On the **sixth** day
of Thanksgiving,
I was thankful for:

Six turkeys gobbling,
Five piles of leaves!
Four golden buckles,
Three fall squash,
Two sacks of apples,
and an evening at home
with family.

On the **seventh** day
of Thanksgiving,
I was thankful for:

Seven sports fans playing,
Six turkeys gobbling,
Five piles of leaves!
Four golden buckles,
Three fall squash,
Two sacks of apples,
and an evening at home
with family.

On the **eighth** day
of Thanksgiving,
I was thankful for:

Eight loved ones hugging,
Seven sports fans playing,
Six turkeys gobbling,
Five piles of leaves!
Four golden buckles,
Three fall squash,
Two sacks of apples,
and an evening at home
with family.

On the **ninth** day
of Thanksgiving,
I was thankful for:

Nine aunts arriving,
Eight loved ones hugging,
Seven sports fans playing,
Six turkeys gobbling,
Five piles of leaves!
Four golden buckles,
Three fall squash,
Two sacks of apples,
and an evening at home
with family.

On the **tenth** day
of Thanksgiving,
I was thankful for:

Ten uncles baking,
Nine aunts arriving,
Eight loved ones hugging,

Seven sports fans playing,
Six turkeys gobbling,
Five piles of leaves!
Four golden buckles,
Three fall squash,
Two sacks of apples,
and an evening at home
with family.

On the **eleventh** day
of Thanksgiving,
I was thankful for:

Eleven hot pies cooling,
Ten uncles baking,
Nine aunts arriving,
Eight loved ones hugging,

Seven sports fans playing,
Six turkeys gobbling,
Five piles of leaves!
Four golden buckles,
Three fall squash,
Two sacks of apples,
and an evening at home
with family.

On the **twelfth** day
of Thanksgiving,
I was thankful for:

Twelve cousins giggling,
Eleven hot pies cooling,
Ten uncles baking,

Nine aunts arriving,
Eight loved ones hugging,
Seven sports fans playing,
Six turkeys gobbling,
Five piles of leaves!
Four golden buckles,
Three fall squash,
Two sacks of apples . . .

. . . and an evening at home with family.

Happy Thanksgiving!